For more than forty years,
Yearling has been the leading name
in classic and award-winning literature
for young readers.

Yearling books feature children's
favorite authors and characters,
providing dynamic stories of adventure,
humor, history, mystery, and fantasy.

Trust Yearling paperbacks to entertain,
inspire, and promote the love of reading
in all children.

OTHER YEARLING BOOKS YOU WILL ENJOY

ENCYCLOPEDIA BROWN

and the Case of the
Slippery Salamander

DONALD J. SOBOL

Illustrated by WARREN CHANG

A YEARLING BOOK

Published by Yearling, an imprint of Random House Children's Books
a division of Random House, Inc., New York

If you purchased this book without a cover you should be aware that this book is
stolen property. It was reported as "unsold and destroyed" to the publisher and neither
the author nor the publisher has received any payment for this "stripped book."

Text copyright © 1999 by Donald J. Sobol
Illustrations copyright © 1999 by Warren Chang

All rights reserved. No part of this book may be reproduced or transmitted in any form
or by any means, electronic or mechanical, including photocopying, recording, or by any
information storage and retrieval system, without the written permission of the publisher,
except where permitted by law. For information address Delacorte Press.

Yearling and the jumping horse design are registered trademarks of Random House, Inc.

Visit us on the Web! www.randomhouse.com/kids

Educators and librarians, for a variety of teaching tools, visit us at
www.randomhouse.com/teachers

ISBN: 0-553-48521-0

Reprinted by arrangement with Delacorte Press

Printed in the United States of America

April 2003

20 19 18 17 16 15 14 13 12 11

Contents

In Memory of Rebecca Blackwell
October 30, 1987–April 25, 1989

The Case of the Slippery Salamander

To a visitor, Idaville looked like an ordinary seaside town. It had churches, two car washes, and three movie theaters. It had bike paths, sparkling white beaches, a synagogue, and plenty of good fishing spots.

But there was something out of the ordinary about Idaville: For more than a year, no child or grown-up had gotten away with breaking a law.

From coast to coast, people wanted to know: How did Idaville do it?

The secret resided in a red brick house at 13 Rover Avenue. That was where Idaville's police chief lived with his wife and son.

Chief Brown was a smart, kind, and brave man.

But he wasn't the one who kept crooks from getting away with their crimes. No, the brains behind it all was his ten-year-old son, Encyclopedia.

Encyclopedia's real name was Leroy. But only his parents and teachers called him that. Everyone else called him "Encyclopedia" because his brain was filled with more facts than a reference book.

Sometimes the Brown family was tempted to tell the world about Encyclopedia's amazing talent as a crime-solver. But so far they hadn't leaked a word. For one thing, the Browns didn't like to boast. For another, who would believe that Idaville's top detective was a fifth-grader?

One Monday night Chief Brown sat at the dinner table, staring at his plate of spaghetti. So far he hadn't slurped up a single strand. Encyclopedia and his mother knew the reason.

The chief wasn't eating because he had come up against a crime that he couldn't solve.

Encyclopedia waited for his dad to tell him about the case. Whenever Chief Brown was stumped, Encyclopedia cracked the case for him, usually by asking just one question.

At last Chief Brown looked up. "There was a theft at the aquarium today," he said, rubbing his forehead.

Last summer an aquarium had opened near the

beach. The most popular attractions were the giant shark tanks, the dolphin shows, and the Den of Darkness.

The Den of Darkness was a huge indoor exhibit of reptiles and amphibians. Encyclopedia especially liked visiting the frogs and salamanders in the amphibian section.

"I hope the great white sharks weren't stolen," Mrs. Brown said with a smile. "That would certainly take a bite out of business!"

Chief Brown shook his head. "It wasn't the sharks."

Encyclopedia put down his fork and listened carefully as his father explained that Fred, a tiger salamander, had been stolen.

"Fred was shipped to the aquarium only two days ago," Chief Brown said. "He was being kept apart from the other animals until the officials were sure he was healthy. If he got a clean bill of health, he was to go on display next month."

"Do you have any clues, dear?" Mrs. Brown asked.

The chief frowned. "Not many. All we know is that the salamander disappeared this morning, sometime between ten-thirty and eleven forty-five."

"Why would someone steal a salamander?" Mrs. Brown wondered.

"Fred is the aquarium's only tiger salamander," her husband explained. "From what the director of the aquarium told me, someone could sell him for a lot of money."

"Really?" Mrs. Brown's eyes widened. "Do you think a visitor might have stolen him?"

"It's very unlikely," Chief Brown replied. "Employees and volunteers are the only ones who have access to the back room in the Den of Darkness where Fred was being kept."

Chief Brown told Encyclopedia and Mrs. Brown that three people had been working at the exhibit that morning: Mrs. King, who volunteered at the aquarium every Monday; Sam Maine, the man in charge of cleaning and maintaining the exhibits; and Dr. O'Donnell, an expert on reptiles and amphibians.

"Did you question the three of them?" Mrs. Brown asked.

· The chief nodded. "Dr. O'Donnell spent the morning examining a new crocodile from Australia. Sam Maine told me he was busy cleaning out exhibits and feeding some of the lizards. Several people saw him working," Chief Brown added, "so it looks like he's telling the truth."

"What about Mrs. King?" his wife prodded.

Chief Brown frowned. "Actually, Sam Maine

seems very suspicious of Mrs. King," he confided. "And after talking with her I can see why. Mrs. King is fascinated with salamanders."

"Fascinated with *salamanders?*" Mrs. Brown echoed.

The chief nodded again. "She told me she has dozens of them at home as pets, and that Fred is the first tiger salamander she's ever seen." He shook his head. "Mrs. King does seem odd—she thinks salamanders are sacred creatures with magical powers."

Encyclopedia spoke up. "In ancient times, people used salamanders for medicine. They also believed that salamanders could eat fire and live in flames."

"Maybe Fred wasn't stolen for money," Mrs. Brown said thoughtfully. "Maybe Mrs. King took Fred just because she thinks he's a special specimen!"

"That's exactly what I've been thinking," Chief Brown admitted. "But there's no proof that Mrs. King had the opportunity to steal Fred. She was with a group of schoolchildren from ten-thirty to eleven-fifteen. After that she went over to the cafeteria for a coffee break. One of the cashiers said he saw her there."

Chief Brown sighed with frustration. "I hate to admit it, but this case has me baffled!"

Encyclopedia closed his eyes. His parents watched him hopefully. They knew that when Encyclopedia closed his eyes, it meant he was doing his deepest thinking.

A moment later Encyclopedia was ready. He opened his eyes and asked his one question:

"Has Sam Maine been working at the aquarium long, Dad?"

"Actually, he was hired only two weeks ago," Chief Brown answered. "But he has a lot of experience. Sam told me he's been taking care of salamanders and other lizards for more than nineteen years."

That was all Encyclopedia needed to hear.

"Oh no he hasn't!" Encyclopedia declared with a satisfied smile. "If he's a lizard expert, then I'm the Queen of England! Sam Maine is lying, and I can prove it!"

How does Encyclopedia know?

(Turn to page 77 for the solution to The Case of the Slippery Salamander.)

The Case of the Banana Burglar

During the school year, Encyclopedia helped his father solve mysteries for the police department. When school closed for summer vacation, he opened his own detective agency in the garage.

Each morning he hung out his sign:

Brown Detective Agency
13 Rover Avenue
LEROY BROWN
President
No case too small
25¢ a day plus expenses

Idaville was in the middle of a heat wave. The thermometer outside Encyclopedia's garage had just hit ninety-six degrees when his first customer arrived. It was Pablo Pizzaro—Idaville's best boy artist.

Pablo's face was bright red, and sweat spotted his blue T-shirt.

"I'm steaming, and it's got nothing to do with the heat!" Pablo declared. "Bugs Meany accused me of stealing a banana! I want to hire you to prove my innocence."

Bugs was the leader of a gang of tough older boys. They called themselves the Tigers. They should have called themselves the Tea Bags. They were always getting into hot water.

"Tell me exactly what happened," Encyclopedia said.

Pablo placed a quarter on the gas can next to Encyclopedia and began to talk.

"Monsieur LeBlanc hired me to be his assistant in the Art in the Park program this summer."

Encyclopedia nodded. Every year Idaville sponsored an arts program for children at the park. Monsieur LeBlanc was famous in Idaville for his beautiful paintings—and for his ugly temper. The peevish painter flew into a rage as often as the wind changed direction.

According to Pablo, this morning the students, including Bugs, had been learning how to paint still-life pictures. Before the first class, Monsieur LeBlanc had placed fruit in a large wooden bowl.

"He picked the fruit himself at an expensive greengrocer in the city. Then he arranged it just so in the bowl," Pablo explained. "Monsieur insisted that there must be exactly the right balance of three apples, two pears, and two bananas."

Encyclopedia waited for Pablo to go on.

"Monsieur taught the first two morning sessions on his own," Pablo said. "After I arrived to help with Session Three, he took a break. When he came back a few minutes later, he noticed that a banana was missing from the bowl."

"So that's when the banana split," cracked Encyclopedia.

"It's no laughing matter!" Pablo cried. "Monsieur LeBlanc thinks I stole it!"

"What makes him think that?" the detective asked.

Pablo was scowling. "Bugs Meany! When Monsieur asked where the banana was, Bugs told him I took it," Pablo continued. "Bugs told Monsieur I thought the students' paintings would look better with just one banana."

"With food in the picture, I should have guessed that Bugs Meany was involved," Encyclopedia muttered.

"Please help me prove that I didn't steal the banana, Encyclopedia," Pablo went on desperately. "If you don't, Monsieur LeBlanc won't give me my job back!"

Encyclopedia agreed to take the case. The two boys headed for South Park.

Because of the heat, the Art in the Park students had been painting inside the Community Center, which was air-conditioned. The center was a large building near the tennis courts in the park. When Encyclopedia walked into the building behind Pablo, he bumped smack into a big boy in a painter's apron.

Encyclopedia did a double take. The boy in the apron was Bugs Meany.

"Well, well, well," Bugs sneered. "If it isn't the sloth who calls himself a sleuth. What are you doing here, snoop-face?"

Encyclopedia ignored the bully's nasty remarks. "I was surprised to hear that you signed up for Art in the Park, Bugs. I didn't think you were the artistic type."

"Us Tigers have a sensitive side, you know. In fact, Monsieur LeBlanc thinks I've got talent,"

Bugs said proudly. "He said I might even be the next Vincent van Goat."

"It's van *Gogh*!" Pablo snapped. "You're an artist, all right, Bugs. A con artist!"

"You two lamebrains are sapping my creative energy," Bugs declared. He tried to push his way past them. "If you'll stop blocking the door, I'd like to go home for lunch. All I've eaten today is a lousy banana."

Encyclopedia stepped aside to let Bugs pass.

"See?" Pablo said. "Bugs practically confessed just now! He stole the banana because he was hungry, and then he blamed the whole thing on me!"

"I'm sure you're right, Pablo," Encyclopedia said. "But what we have to do is find some proof."

The art students were painting inside a large, sunny room in the Community Center. The room was filled with jars of paint, brushes, paper, and other art supplies.

Six or seven students stood before easels, brushes in hand. They were painting a bowl of fruit that sat on a table in the front of the room.

Monsieur LeBlanc glared when he saw Pablo. "I thought I told you that you were fired!"

Encyclopedia spoke up quickly. "We're here to investigate the banana theft, Monsieur LeBlanc. If

13

you don't mind, sir," he added politely, "we'd like to look around for a few minutes."

Encyclopedia thought the angry artist was going to say no. But before Monsieur could reply, a student raised his hand and asked for help.

"You may look around!" Monsieur LeBlanc snapped as he went over to help the student. "But only for a moment. And do not disturb any of my students!"

Encyclopedia tiptoed to the front of the room to examine the bowl of fruit. Next he headed for a clothesline strung across the back of the room. Several dozen still-life paintings were clipped to the line. When Encyclopedia looked at them more closely, he noticed that the paint was still wet.

"These paintings are from the earlier classes today, right?" he whispered to Pablo, who was nervously following him around the room.

"That's right," Pablo whispered back. "The pictures on the left are from the first session. The ones on the right were painted by the students in Session Two."

Encyclopedia saw that the pictures from Session One showed a still life of seven pieces of fruit. When Encyclopedia went to look at the paintings from Session Two, Monsieur LeBlanc stormed over to him.

"That is enough!" the artist declared. "You are disturbing my students!" He narrowed his eyes at Pablo. "This investigation is pointless! Pablo is the thief!"

"Please believe me, Monsieur," Pablo said. "I didn't take the banana. And I—"

"*Silence!*" Monsieur LeBlanc bellowed, waving his arms. "The banana was here this morning, and it disappeared after you arrived. You ruined my perfect arrangement of fruit!"

Encyclopedia decided to intervene before Monsieur LeBlanc threw one of his world-famous temper tantrums.

"Bugs Meany took the banana and blamed Pablo, Monsieur," he said quickly. "I have proof."

"Proof, schmoof! As you Americans like to say"—he pointed a finger at Pablo—"the proof is in the pudding!"

"Not this time," Encyclopedia said calmly. "This time the proof is in the *paintings*."

What did Encyclopedia mean?

(Turn to page 78 for the solution to The Case of the Banana Burglar.)

The Case of the Dead Cockroach

Bugs Meany hated being outsmarted by Encyclopedia all the time. At night he dreamed about ways to put out the detective's lights.

But Bugs's sweet dreams of revenge came to an end as soon as he remembered his worst nightmare—a nightmare named Sally Kimball.

Sally was Encyclopedia's junior partner in the detective agency. She was also the best athlete and the prettiest girl in fifth grade. But all Bugs remembered about Sally was how quick she was with her fists. More than once Sally had knocked him down faster than Bugs could say, "I'm a big bully."

"I'm telling you, Encyclopedia," Sally warned

the detective one afternoon, "Bugs won't rest until he gets revenge."

The two detectives were on their way to the Tigers' clubhouse. Bugs had just called to ask them to come to an important meeting.

Encyclopedia shrugged. "On the phone it sounded as if Bugs really needs our help. Maybe he's finally turned over a new leaf."

"You mean he's crawled out from *under* a leaf," Sally said. "I still think we'd better be careful."

The Tigers' clubhouse was in an unused toolshed behind Mr. Sweeny's auto body shop. Bugs was inside with two other Tigers, Duke Kelly and Spike Larsen. The three of them were talking about Idaville's Annual Insect Race.

When Encyclopedia and Sally arrived, Bugs looked up with a smirk.

"Speaking of insects . . . it's the clueless sleuth and his simpleminded sidekick."

"Watch it, beetle brain!" Sally snarled. She stepped up to Bugs and shoved her fist under his nose. "One more crack like that and I'll whip you like a pint of heavy cream!"

Bugs smiled weakly. "Wh-What's the matter, Sally?" he stammered. "Can't you take a little joke?"

"Not from you," Sally shot back. She removed her fist, but she was still glowering at him.

"What's up, Bugs?" Encyclopedia asked. "What is this meeting about, anyway?"

"I want to hire you two for an important job," the Tigers' leader said.

"What kind of job?" Encyclopedia asked curiously.

Bugs showed him a cardboard shoe box with dozens of small holes in its lid. "The Annual Insect Race is this Saturday, and I have to go out of town for a few days."

"He wants to hire you to be his bug's bodyguard while he's gone," said Spike.

Sally looked at Bugs suspiciously. "Why does your bug need a bodyguard?" she demanded.

"He's very fast," Bugs bragged. "I'm afraid someone will try to steal him before Saturday."

"He's a champion cockroach from Madagascar," Duke informed them proudly.

Bugs lifted the lid and showed the detectives the roach inside. He was a big bug with a shiny brown shell.

"My roach is competing against a beetle and a scorpion on Saturday," Bugs said. "I'm sure he'll win."

"Why'd you call us for the job?" Sally wanted to know.

Bugs shrugged. "You may be snoops, but I trust you to guard my bug like he was one of your own. Don't worry—I'll pay you for your services."

Sally looked doubtful, but Encyclopedia didn't see the harm in accepting Bugs's offer. "We'll take the job," he replied.

Bugs handed over a quarter, and Encyclopedia picked up the shoe box.

"The race is being held at the main pavilion at South Park," Bugs said. "Meet me there on Saturday a few minutes before ten."

As they walked away, Sally shook her head. "I hope you know what you're doing, Encyclopedia."

"I know what I'm doing, Sally," the detective replied calmly.

On Saturday morning, Encyclopedia and Sally arrived at the park early with Bugs's bug. When Encyclopedia lifted the shoe box lid to check on him, he saw the roach crawling around inside.

Sally looked around. "Where's Bugs?"

"We're twenty minutes early," Encyclopedia replied. "He's probably not here yet."

A huge banner was hanging from the pavilion:

IDAVILLE'S ANNUAL INSECT RACE—TODAY! A crowd of spectators had already gathered there.

"There's one of the roach's competitors," Sally said, pointing to a glass jar in a blond girl's hand. Inside the jar was a big black scorpion.

"I wouldn't want to get too close to that fellow," Sally remarked.

The girl heard her. "Don't worry. He doesn't sting."

The other contestant was a green beetle owned by a boy with red hair and freckles.

Encyclopedia looked over the other racers carefully. "Roaches are pretty fast," he said. "I hate to say it, but I think Bugs might actually have a winner with this cockroach."

Encyclopedia watched the judges set up a small ring on the concrete floor. Then they explained the rules: At the start of the race, the insects would be placed in the center of the large ring. The first bug to reach the wall around the ring was the winner.

At two minutes to ten, Bugs hurried up to Encyclopedia.

"Quick! Hand over my roach," he said, grabbing the shoe box away from Encyclopedia. "He's got to do his warm-ups before the race."

"Warm-ups?" Sally laughed. "You've got to be kidding!"

Bugs gave her a nasty look. "You knuckleheads don't know anything about champion bug-racing," he retorted. "For your information, I've trained my bug to see himself speeding across the finish line before every race."

Encyclopedia didn't bother to hide his smile.

Neither did Sally. "You're even dumber than I thought you were, Bugs!" she exclaimed, hooting with laughter. "You actually think that works?"

"Laugh all you want," Bugs snarled. "But how do you think my roach got to be number one?"

Encyclopedia watched Bugs carry the box over to a quiet spot a few feet away. Keeping his back to the crowd, Bugs murmured a few soothing words as he lifted the lid of the shoe box.

Sally was still laughing and shaking her head. "Can you believe that? Bugs Meany thinks he can train a bug to see himself winning a race! Maybe he can teach it to fetch his slippers, too!"

"Or better yet, to do his homework," Encyclopedia joined in.

Sally was about to add another wisecrack when a loud wail rose from a short distance away.

"My roach!" Bugs cried. "He's dead!" Bugs pointed an accusing finger at Sally and Encyclopedia. "I left my champion insect in the care of those two cold-blooded creeps and they murdered him!"

A startled murmur rippled through the crowd.

"What are you talking about, Bugs?" Sally demanded. "That roach was fine five minutes ago!"

"See for yourself!" Bugs replied, holding the box out to the crowd. He rubbed his eye as if wiping away a tear as he added, "My poor roach. He's deader than a doornail!"

Encyclopedia walked over and looked inside the box. Sure enough, the big brown roach was just sitting there, motionless. Even when Encyclopedia reached in to touch his shiny brown back, the bug didn't move. Bugs was telling the truth—the roach was dead.

"I told you!" Bugs declared. He waved over one of the judges. "Call nine-one-one! These two monsters should be locked up before they harm some more innocent insects!"

Encyclopedia shook his head. "Sally was right about you, Bugs. You asked us to baby-sit your bug so that you could set us up. You switched the live roach with a dead one to make it look as if he died in our care."

Bugs looked offended. "I'd never do something like that," he said to the judges.

"You might as well confess, Bugs," Encyclopedia told him. "Because while you were planning your roach's funeral, you overlooked one very important fact!"

What did Encyclopedia notice about the bug?

(Turn to page 79 for the solution to The Case of the Dead Cockroach.)

The Case of the Roman-Numeral Robber

Encyclopedia's friends Charlie Stewart and Herb Stein liked to fish near the new marina at Coconut Bay. Encyclopedia often went with them.

Late one afternoon the three boys headed home with their fishing gear. It had been a good day for two of the fishermen. Charlie had caught five bluefish, and Herb had reeled in a flounder. But Encyclopedia's pail was empty.

"It's too bad you didn't catch anything, Encyclopedia," Herb said as they turned onto Coconut Boulevard.

"Maybe next time you'll have better luck," Charlie added.

"Thanks," Encyclopedia said. "I hope so."

As they walked along the busy street, Encyclopedia noticed some construction workers knocking down an old office building. Across the street, several fancy shops and a restaurant had replaced an old supermarket.

"I didn't realize so many new businesses had moved into this neighborhood," Encyclopedia remarked to his friends.

Suddenly there was a loud shout. A man rushed out of a nearby store. "Help! I've been robbed!" he yelled frantically.

The three boys raced over.

"What happened, sir?" Encyclopedia asked.

"My jewelry store!" the man gasped, pointing at the building behind him. "I left it for just a few minutes, and while I was gone, someone broke in!"

It was a run-down two-story building. A sign above the faded green awning read VON MARTIN'S FINE JEWELRY.

"Are you Mr. von Martin?" Charlie asked.

The man nodded. Herb asked him what had been stolen.

"The robber took the most precious item in the store," Mr. von Martin replied. "A diamond wristwatch worth about four thousand dollars."

"Four thousand dollars?" Herb gasped. "And my mother says *her* time is valuable!"

"The watch is worth much more than that to me," Mr. von Martin said. "My family has been in the jewelry business for generations. The watch was designed by my great-grandfather over a hundred years ago."

Mr. von Martin took a handkerchief out of his pocket and wiped his brow. "The thief—whoever he is—left me a note."

"He did?" Encyclopedia said. "I bet he's the Roman-Numeral Robber."

"Who?" Charlie asked.

Mr. von Martin peered at Encyclopedia in confusion. "I don't know what you're talking about, young man."

Encyclopedia explained that there had been several other robberies near the marina recently. In each case, the thief had left behind a note. According to Chief Brown, and according to what Encyclopedia had read in the newspaper, the police were calling the thief the Roman-Numeral Robber.

"Why do they call him that?" asked Herb.

"He uses Roman numerals instead of Arabic numerals in his notes," Encyclopedia replied. He turned to Mr. von Martin. "Have you called the police yet?"

"Not yet," the jeweler admitted. "I was so upset, I wasn't thinking. But I'd better do that right away."

Encyclopedia and his friends followed the man into the store. While Mr. von Martin made the call, Charlie whispered to Encyclopedia: "What are Roman numerals?"

"I'll show you." Encyclopedia took a pen and a pad of paper from his backpack.

"These are the Arabic figures for one through ten." On the pad, Encyclopedia had written:

1 2 3 4 5 6 7 8 9 10

"And these are the Roman numerals for one through ten." Encyclopedia showed Charlie the following:

I II III IV V VI VII VIII IX X

"They may be Roman numerals, but they're Greek to me!" Charlie cracked.

The boys looked around the shop. It was dark and musty. Several long glass display cases lined the walls. Near the cash register was a wrinkled copy of that day's *Idaville News*, an unopened can of soda, and a bag of pretzels.

When the jeweler returned from the back

room, Encyclopedia asked him where the stolen watch had been.

Mr. von Martin pointed to a velvet tray also near the cash register. "Right there," he said. "I was cleaning the watch before I went out. Since I was only going to be gone for a few minutes, I didn't bother to lock it up. But I did lock the front door."

Herb pointed to a broken window toward the rear of the store. "The thief must have gotten in through there."

Encyclopedia asked to see the note from the thief. The jeweler handed over a small sheet of paper.

June XXIIII
Dear Mr. von Martin:
Say good-bye forever to your precious von Martin watch. I am sure that it will bring me a small fortune when I sell it!

Encyclopedia stared at the note, thinking hard.

A few minutes later, two police officers hurried into the jewelry store. Encyclopedia recognized them as Officer Lopez and her partner, Officer Brady. Officer Lopez was carrying a fingerprinting kit.

Encyclopedia hurried over to the policewoman. "Don't bother dusting the store for fingerprints, Officer Lopez," he whispered. "The watch wasn't stolen by the Roman-Numeral Robber—Mr. von Martin just wants us to *think* it was."

The officer looked startled. "Are you sure, Encyclopedia?"

"I'm positive. Mr. von Martin hid the watch, then wrote the note himself," the detective explained.

Why is Encyclopedia so sure?

(Turn to page 80 for the solution to The Case of the Roman-Numeral Robber.)

The Case of the Runaway Judge

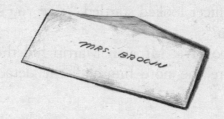

Mrs. Brown

When Encyclopedia came downstairs for breakfast the next morning, his mother was on the phone. Encyclopedia could tell by her expression that she was upset about something.

"I should have known Ms. Wedgwood would do something like this," Mrs. Brown murmured after she hung up the receiver.

"What's wrong, Mom?" Encyclopedia asked.

Mrs. Brown sighed. "That was the innkeeper at the Blue Point Inn. He told me one of the judges from the Idaville Flower Show got married last night. She met a rose grower from Bloomington, and they eloped in the middle of the night."

"What's wrong with that?" Encyclopedia asked.

"She left before announcing the winner in her category," Mrs. Brown said. "She was supposed to name the winner at a press conference at two o'clock this afternoon. The innkeeper said she left an envelope in the room. I do hope it has the winner's name inside."

"Oh." Encyclopedia poured himself a bowl of Rice Crunchies and sat down at the table.

Mrs. Brown had taught English and other subjects at the high school. During summer vacation, she helped to organize the Annual Idaville Flower Show. The show drew hundreds of talented gardeners from all over the state.

"What was Ms. Wedgwood's category?" Encyclopedia asked his mother.

"Garden mazes," replied Mrs. Brown. She explained that this was a new category at the flower show.

"Since no one in the club knows anything about garden mazes, we had to hire Ms. Wedgwood. She's very unusual, but she's a landscape architect and an expert on English garden mazes."

"What do you mean, she's very unusual?" Encyclopedia asked.

"Before Ms. Wedgwood became a landscape architect, she worked at a dozen different jobs," Mrs. Brown said. "She was a waitress, a code breaker for the Army, a circus clown, a garbage collector, a jeweler, a toll collector. . . . Not only that, this is the fifth time in seven years that she's been married."

"Wow." Encyclopedia grinned. "She does sound unusual!"

"Still, she came highly recommended," Mrs. Brown went on. "I'm very surprised that she'd leave before finishing her job as judge. I really do hope the name of the winner is in that envelope."

Encyclopedia offered to go with his mother to the inn. Thirty minutes later, they parked in front of the building.

The Blue Point Inn was a rambling white house with fourteen guest rooms, and a restaurant on the ground floor. Colorful flowers were in bloom all over the grounds.

The innkeeper, Mr. Crawford, was at the front desk. "Ms. Wedgwood's mind was definitely on romance when she left," he told them. "The woman who cleans the rooms said Ms. Wedgwood forgot to pack a couple of things."

"May I see the envelope she left for me, Mr. Crawford?" Mrs. Brown asked politely.

"Certainly," he replied. "We have a reception in the restaurant this afternoon, so I asked the maid to finish cleaning Ms. Wedgwood's room later. The letter is still in the room."

The innkeeper gave Encyclopedia and Mrs. Brown the key, and they headed to Room 10 on the second floor.

Inside, Encyclopedia gazed around in wonder. It was a large room, with pale pink carpeting and white wicker furniture. Thrown across the couch was a red dress. On the table was a pocket-size calendar open to January.

"There it is!" Mrs. Brown exclaimed. An envelope with her name written on it was propped against a lamp. She quickly ripped it open and read the letter aloud:

> **Dear Mrs. Brown,**
> **I am deeply sorry that I was not able to be here in person to announce the name of the winner in the garden maze category. My life has taken an unexpected—but quite wonderful—turn.**
> **By the time you read this, my new husband and I will be on our honeymoon on a small island off the coast of Scotland. I'm afraid that the island has no phone service so it will be impossible to reach me.**

Please give the talented gardener a hearty congratulations.
Sincerely,
Ida Wedgwood

"So who's the winner, Mom?" Encyclopedia asked.

"I don't know, Leroy." Mrs. Brown frowned as she scanned the letter again. "Ms. Wedgwood didn't write down the winner's name!"

Encyclopedia gazed around the room, thinking hard. "Do you have a list of the gardeners who entered the maze contest, Mom?" he asked.

"Actually, I do. Ms. Wedgwood gave me the names of the finalists the other day." His mother fumbled in her purse for a moment before pulling out a handwritten list of six names.

Encyclopedia quickly looked them over.

Nicholas Chin
Karyn Meyers
Candace Flintoff
Roberta Garnet
Alexander Findlay
Melissa Abruzzo

"Didn't you say that Ms. Wedgwood used to work as a jeweler and as a code breaker, Mom?" Encyclopedia asked.

"Yes," Mrs. Brown said with a sigh. "I hope she was more responsible when she worked at those jobs. I can't imagine what she was thinking last night when she left without leaving me the winner's name."

"You know what, Mom?" Encyclopedia said slowly. "I think she *did* leave you the winner's name."

His mother looked at him sharply. "What do you mean, Leroy?"

"As you said, Mom, Ms. Wedgwood is very unusual," Encyclopedia told her. "She left the name in code."

Encyclopedia pointed to a name on the list. "The winner in the maze category is—"

Who is the winner?

(Turn to page 82 for the solution to The Case of the Runaway Judge.)

The Case of the Peacock's Egg

"Encyclopedia!"

One Thursday afternoon Jack Connor hurried into the Browns' garage. Encyclopedia saw that his six-year-old neighbor was carefully holding a large egg.

Jack reached into his pocket with his free hand and pulled out a coin. "I want to hire you," he said, putting a quarter on the gas can. "I think Wilford Wiggins has cheated me out of my birthday money!"

"Not Wilford again," Encyclopedia groaned.

Wilford was a high-school dropout. He spent his mornings lying in bed. He was so lazy that he couldn't stand to watch people work before noon.

Most of his time was spent thinking up ways to cheat little kids out of their savings.

"What's Wilford up to this time?" Encyclopedia asked.

Jack held up the egg. "He sold this to me last week. He swore if I took good care of the egg, it would hatch into a beautiful peacock with colorful feathers."

"Wilford Wiggins lies like a rug," Encyclopedia remarked in disgust.

"You're telling me!" the younger boy exclaimed. "Wilford said it would take only five days for this egg to hatch. But I've waited a whole week and nothing has happened. I want to stop that crook before more kids shell out their savings."

Encyclopedia took the egg from Jack and checked it carefully. It was large, and its shell was light brown.

"I have a feeling Wilford's story is full of cracks," he said, returning the egg to Jack. "I'll take the case."

Jack reached into his pocket again and pulled out a crumpled blue flyer. He showed it to Encyclopedia. "Wilford is trying to sell more eggs right now."

Encyclopedia read the flyer.

CALLING ALL PEACOCK ADMIRERS!
For a limited time only, rare and valuable peacock eggs are for sale. Your special egg is guaranteed to hatch into a beautiful peacock in just five days.

For more information, contact Mr. Wilford Wiggins. Or, if you don't want to risk missing this special offer, meet him in person at the entrance to Sunny Spot Farm on Thursday at 1 P.M.

Encyclopedia glanced at his watch. It was nearly one o'clock. "If we bike to Sunny Spot Farm, we'll make it in time to stop Wilford."

Sunny Spot Farm was about a mile from the Browns' house. When Encyclopedia and Jack arrived, Wilford Wiggins was standing near the long gravel driveway leading to the farm. A large group of children was standing around listening to his sales pitch.

"Step right up and get your *gen-u-ine* peacock's eggs! For just fifteen-ninety-nine, you, too, can be the owner of a real, live peacock! Your bird's amazing plumage is sure to dazzle your friends and family."

A girl with long brown hair raised her hand. "Can you tell us where you got the peacock eggs?"

"Of course, little lady." Wilford's lips curled

into a smile as he jerked his thumb at the farm behind him. "These eggs are from Idaville's own Sunny Spot Farm."

A boy standing near Encyclopedia looked suspicious. "Oh yeah? I've been to Sunny Spot Farm dozens of times, and I've never seen any peacocks here."

Wilford lowered his voice. "These are extremely rare birds, Joey. They're kept in a special pen, and only fine peacock collectors such as myself have been allowed to see them."

"What's so special about them?" another boy called out.

"Their feathers are very colorful," Wilford answered. "In fact, the peacock who laid these eggs had the most beautiful feathers I've ever seen."

With that, Wilford held up the basket of eggs. "Now, who would like to buy one for just four ninety-nine?"

Several children in the crowd waved bills at Wilford.

"You've got to do something, Encyclopedia," Jack whispered. "Wilford's going to cheat those kids too!"

"Don't worry, Jack." Encyclopedia patted the younger boy on the shoulder. "He's not going to get away with anything."

The detective marched up to the egg salesman. "Not so fast, Wilford!"

Wilford looked up, startled. But then he smiled. "Why, Encyclopedia," he cooed. "Don't tell me you're trying to stop these dear children from buying pet peacocks?"

"I hate to ruffle your feathers, Wilford, but that's exactly what I'm doing," Encyclopedia said. "You've fouled up your fowls for the last time!"

What does Encyclopedia mean?

(Turn to page 83 for the solution to The Case of the Peacock's Egg.)

The Case of the Umpire's Error

It was the night of the championship baseball game between the Idaville Indians and the Pittfield Porpoises.

When Encyclopedia and Sally entered South Park, the bright lights over the baseball diamond were on. A big crowd had already filled the bleachers.

Sally was wearing her blue Indians T-shirt. "The Indians are going to wallop the Porpoises tonight!" she said, rubbing her hands gleefully.

"I hope the Indians win, but the Porpoises are favored," Encyclopedia replied. "They have the best record in the league."

"But the Indians have Tara Padrowski," Sally reminded him.

Tara Padrowski was a home run–hitting sensation. All summer long the local papers had been filled with stories about how the power hitter had hit more home runs than anyone else in the league. Encyclopedia hoped they'd get to see her hit one out of the park tonight.

Encyclopedia and Sally found seats right behind the Indians' Bench. On the field, the Idaville players were warming up. When Tara Padrowski stepped up to the plate to take a practice swing, she hit the ball so hard, it rocketed over the fence.

"That was a home run, and this is only practice!" Sally cheered.

Mr. Padrowski stood up and took a bow. "That's my daughter!" he shouted. "Did you see her smack that ball out of the park? She's going to blow the Porpoises' socks off!"

A few parents in the Porpoises' section glared at him.

"Oh yeah?" a Porpoise fan shouted at Mr. Padrowski. "Well, my grandmother could hit your pitcher's best stuff!"

Encyclopedia listened as the adults continued trading insults.

"The parents seem pretty uptight about this game," he finally said to Sally.

She nodded. "I heard that last week during the play-offs, three fathers had to leave the park because they were disrupting the game."

"Really?" Encyclopedia shook his head. "I know it's the championship and everything, but it's still just a game."

On the field, the players' warm-up had ended several minutes ago.

"Why hasn't the game started yet?" Sally asked.

"Something must be up," Encyclopedia replied. He noticed the Indians' coach talking with the Porpoises' coach. Both men looked worried.

"What's going on?" Encyclopedia asked a player on the bench.

"The umpire had car trouble on his way to the field," the player explained. "They've been calling around for a substitute ump, but everyone's away. If they can't find someone to fill in, we'll have to postpone the game."

One of the fathers in the Porpoises' section overheard their conversation. He jumped to his feet and waved to the coaches. "I can fill in!"

"Really?" The Indians' coach looked at him. "You've worked as an ump before, sir?"

"I sure have," the man replied confidently. "I was an umpire in the major leagues for three years before I became a computer salesman."

"Okay, Mr. Payne," the Porpoises' coach replied. "You've got yourself a job."

The Indians' coach found an umpire's mask and pads. Mr. Payne put on the equipment, and a minute later the game finally began.

The Indians took the lead in the bottom of the first inning when Tara Padrowski hit a two-run homer out of the park.

"Tara is hot tonight!" Sally exclaimed.

But by the sixth inning, Encyclopedia was getting worried. The Idaville Indians were losing 5 to 2.

The worst part was, Encyclopedia had the feeling that the substitute umpire was making bad calls against the Indians on purpose.

In the fourth inning, he had thrown out Jimmy Rivera, who was trying to steal second base. Jimmy had looked safe to Encyclopedia and Sally. And after Tara's two-run homer, the ump started calling three strikes on her every time she was up.

Now Tara stood on deck, getting ready for her next turn at bat.

"He's no pitcher. . . . He's no pitcher. . . . ," someone in the Indians' section chanted.

"Keep your eye on the ball, Tara!" her father shouted.

Before Tara stepped over to the plate, the umpire bent down to dust it off. Encyclopedia noticed the words DON'T GO WRONG . . . BUY A KRUMM COMPUTER on the back of his blue T-shirt.

"Maybe the ump will finally give Tara a break and let her get on base," Sally said.

"I hope so," Encyclopedia replied. "I don't think the Indians can win this game if she doesn't get a hit soon."

The first pitch was high. Tara didn't swing.

"Good eye, Tara!" yelled her father.

But the umpire didn't see it that way. "*Str-r-r-rike!*" he called out.

"Are you blind?" Sally shot up from her seat. "That ball was as high as the moon!"

"Get a pair of glasses, Ump!" someone else yelled.

Tara glared at the umpire, shuffling her feet in the dirt.

The next pitch came in high again, and the

ump called another strike. But Tara didn't lose her cool until the third pitch came in wide and low.

"*Str-r-r-ike three!* You're out!"

Tara threw down her bat and stalked over to her coach. "You've got to do something about that ump, Coach! He's trying to make us lose the game!"

Coach Anderson stormed over to the umpire, fuming. "I thought you said you knew how to call a game!"

The umpire lifted his mask and glared at the coach. "You'd better stay out of this, Coach!" he shouted back. "In the major leagues, managers get thrown out for insults like that."

"He's the worst umpire I've ever seen," Sally said glumly. She sank back onto the bench. "It would be one thing if the Indians lost the championship because they weren't playing well. But if they lose because of his bad calls . . ."

"The fans will go nuts," Encyclopedia said.

He kept his eye on the umpire as the man bent down to dust off the plate for the next Indians batter. As Encyclopedia read the words on the back of the man's T-shirt again, something clicked in his mind.

"We've got to stop the game, Sally! That man never worked as an umpire before. He's a major-league liar!"

How did Encyclopedia know?

(Turn to page 84 for the solution to The Case of the Umpire's Error.)

The Case of the Calculating Kid

With the temperature in the nineties, Encyclopedia and Sally decided to beat the heat by heading to the Convention Center. It was air-conditioned.

The National Boat and Fishing Show had opened there. Encyclopedia liked looking at all the fancy boats and fishing equipment for sale.

The two detectives started on the top floor. They roamed around for a long time looking at motorboats, kayaks, and canoes.

The sailboats and bigger boats were displayed on the ground floor. Booths selling fishing gear and boating supplies had been set up there too.

Sally went to look at a large yacht. Encyclopedia stopped at a nearby booth with a sign that said

SHELLS AND MORE SHELLS. The booth sold rare sea-shells from around the world and objects decorated with shells.

Encyclopedia was looking at a mussel-shell soap dish when Sally waved him over.

"Check out this boat, Encyclopedia!" Sally exclaimed, pointing to the enormous yacht. The yacht's name, *Amazing Grace*, was painted on her side. "She has a rec room, a large-screen TV, two Ping-Pong tables, and a hot tub. I would love to cruise around the world on this!"

Encyclopedia was about to remind his partner that she got seasick after a few minutes aboard a canoe. But just then, a salesman approached. His name tag read:

Ron
The Ship-Shape Company

"*Amazing Grace* is a beauty, isn't she?" he said proudly.

"How much does she cost?" Sally asked.

"She's not for sale anymore," Ron replied. "I sold her yesterday. In fact, I wrapped up the paperwork this morning."

Encyclopedia was curious. "Who bought the yacht?"

"Maury and Estelle Hinton bought it," the salesman answered. "They want to cruise around the Greek islands with their nine-year-old son. They paid over a million dollars for it. Can you believe that?"

"Wow." Sally let out a low whistle. "That's a lot of money."

"It sure is, and I'll tell you kids something," Ron went on. "Not everyone could handle a big sale like that. If I weren't such a good salesman . . ."

Ten minutes later, Encyclopedia and Sally finally managed to escape the talkative salesman.

"Whew!" Sally stifled a yawn. "I thought he was going to brag about selling that boat all day long."

"Me too," Encyclopedia agreed. "He sure likes to talk."

As they started down the aisle toward the sailboats, Encyclopedia spotted his father. Chief Brown was writing in a small notebook as he spoke with a tall, well-dressed man. The man had an arm around a woman who was weeping.

"Dad!" Encyclopedia hurried over. "Is everything okay?"

"Hello, Leroy." Chief Brown spoke quietly and his expression was grim. "This is Mr. and Mrs.

Hinton. Their son was kidnapped from the convention center a short while ago."

"Oh, no!" Sally exclaimed.

Encyclopedia instantly recognized the name. "You're the couple who bought *Amazing Grace*, right?"

"That's right," Mr. Hinton said with a scowl. "Thanks to that loudmouth salesman from the Ship-Shape Company, everyone in the convention center knows we bought that boat!"

Mrs. Hinton nodded as she dabbed at her eyes with a tissue. "We think that's why our son was kidnapped. Someone must have heard Ron talking about how much we paid for *Amazing Grace*."

Encyclopedia listened closely as his father filled in more details about the case.

The Hintons had come to the convention center first thing that morning to finish signing the papers to buy the boat. While they were busy, their nine-year-old son, Kent, sat by himself in an empty office.

"He had a pad of paper and his calculator with him," Mr. Hinton said. "Kent is a math genius, and he's always been able to amuse himself for hours with his calculator."

"He loves to solve problems and play tricks

with that thing," Mrs. Hinton added, bursting into tears again.

"Now, now, honey." Her husband patted her shoulder.

"When the Hintons went to collect Kent, he was gone," Chief Brown finished. "An hour later, they discovered that a ransom note had been left for them at the Message Center—the kidnapper is demanding two million dollars for Kent's return."

Sally gasped at the huge figure.

Encyclopedia offered to help, then asked his father to lead him to the office where Kent had been waiting for his parents.

As the Hintons had described, it was a small, bare office just off the main floor of the convention center. The only furniture was a metal desk and a chair. A blank white pad and a calculator sat in the middle of the desk.

Chief Brown explained that since the office was a crime scene, nothing in it had been touched or moved.

"Is that Kent's?" Encyclopedia asked, pointing to the calculator.

Kent's parents nodded.

"It was left behind, with the power still on," Chief Brown said.

Encyclopedia went behind the desk and looked at the calculator. It was a new and very expensive model that could perform lots of fancy functions. When he looked at the display screen, he noticed a series of numbers—577345.

Sally scratched her head. "I wonder what Kent was calculating."

Encyclopedia looked at her, still thinking.

"I know what Kent was calculating!" he burst out a moment later. "He was counting on someone to read the numbers from the *front* of the desk, not behind it!"

What does Encyclopedia mean?

(Turn to page 85 for the solution to The Case of the Calculating Kid.)

The Case of the Presidential Auction

"**T**hree down is a nine-letter word for a fraud or a faker," Sally said to Encyclopedia.

The two detectives were working on the crossword puzzle in *The Idaville News*. Yesterday it had taken them only seven minutes and forty-two seconds to finish the puzzle. Today they were trying to beat their own record.

"That's easy," Encyclopedia replied. " 'Charlatan.' "

Sally wrote down the answer. "Speaking of a nine-letter word for a faker, Gwendolyn is having an auction today."

"I heard," Encyclopedia replied. "And since it's

almost the Fourth of July, she's auctioning off stuff that used to belong to U.S. presidents."

"That's what she claims, anyway," Sally said in a disgusted tone.

Gwendolyn Harris was an eighth-grader who collected antiques. At least that was what she called the stuff that she picked out of people's trash. About once a month Gwendolyn auctioned off the junk. Somehow she managed to trick people into thinking that her "antiques" were worth something.

Encyclopedia was reading the clue for sixteen across when two of his best pals, Benny Breslin and Charlie Stewart, burst into the garage.

"Guess what!" Benny said. He proudly held up a red bow tie. "I just bought a bow tie that used to belong to Harry S. Truman. I'm giving it to my mother for her birthday."

Sally scowled. "Don't tell me, let me guess— Gwendolyn said it's an antique worth thousands of dollars."

"Well, it's not worth that much yet," Benny informed her. "But Gwendolyn says that if my mom holds on to it for a few more years, it'll pay for her retirement!"

Encyclopedia looked at Charlie. "I hope *you*

didn't buy anything from Gwendolyn," he said.

"I sure did!" Charlie held up an old pair of black flip-flops. "I bought Ronald Reagan's beach shoes. He used to wear them when he was governor of California."

Benny finally noticed the suspicious looks on the detectives' faces. "You think we've been conned?"

"Let me put it this way, Benny," Encyclopedia said with a frown. "I have the feeling that bow tie is as genuine as a three-dollar bill."

"Oh, no!" Benny moaned, slapping a hand to his forehead. "I can't believe it! I can't give my mom a phony bow tie for her birthday. You've got to help me and Charlie get our money back, Encyclopedia!"

"I'd like nothing more," Encyclopedia informed his friends.

Fifteen minutes later, Encyclopedia and Sally arrived at Gwendolyn's house. The Presidential Auction was still under way. A large group of kids and adults was gathered around the Harrises' front porch. It was so hot, several of them stood under umbrellas or fanned themselves with sheets of paper.

Encyclopedia spotted Gwendolyn on the top step. She was holding up a plastic pink flamingo.

"Do I hear three dollars, folks?" she called. "Just three dollars for this pink plastic flamingo that Richard Milhous Nixon used to decorate the White House lawn."

A boy raised his hand. "Three dollars," he called.

"Five!" a lady up front shouted.

"I'll give you ten," a man chimed in.

"Going . . . going . . . gone!" Gwendolyn shouted. "The pink flamingo is sold to the man in the blue-and-white shirt."

As the man raced over to get the flamingo, Sally clenched her teeth. "We've got to stop her, Encyclopedia," she muttered. "This auction is a disgrace to our nation's history."

"I agree," Encyclopedia replied. "I'm just waiting till she slips up somehow."

In the next few minutes, Gwendolyn auctioned off a belt buckle that she said belonged to Thomas Jefferson, a Frisbee that she claimed came from John F. Kennedy's summer home on Cape Cod, and a plastic cup that Jimmy Carter had supposedly used as a container for peanuts.

Then Gwendolyn held up an old toothbrush.

Most of its bristles were missing. The ones that remained looked gray and dingy.

Gwendolyn smiled proudly. "I've been saving the best for last," she told the crowd. "Believe it or not, this very ordinary, humble-looking toothbrush belonged to George Washington when he was President."

Several people in the crowd gasped.

"Now that's what I call a real antique!" a man declared. "I'll give you fifty dollars for that, little lady."

Gwendolyn beamed. "Do I hear one hundred dollars?" she asked.

"One hundred dollars!" someone shouted.

Sally elbowed Encyclopedia hard. "You'd better do something fast before Gwendolyn bankrupts this crowd!"

Encyclopedia was already on the move. He calmly stepped forward and held up his hand. "If you were president, you'd be impeached for lying, Gwendolyn. I don't know who used to own that toothbrush, but it wasn't George Washington."

"Oh yeah?" Gwendolyn put her hands on her hips and loomed over Encyclopedia. "And what makes you a presidential scholar, Shorty?"

Encyclopedia looked Gwendolyn directly in the eye as he spoke. "I cannot tell a lie: You forgot one important fact about the Father of our Country."

What was Gwendolyn's mistake?

(Turn to page 86 for the solution to The Case of the Presidential Auction.)

The Case of the Stolen Surfboard

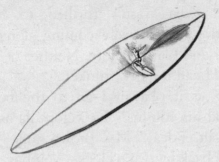

Idaville's heat wave still hadn't broken by the Fourth of July.

"It's going to be another scorcher," Chief Brown said when Encyclopedia came down for breakfast.

"I'll say," Encyclopedia agreed. Looking out the window, he could see that the thermometer near the garage already read seventy-eight degrees.

After breakfast, the phone rang. It was Encyclopedia's pal Benny Breslin.

"Guess what, Encyclopedia!" Benny said excitedly. "I got a new surfboard yesterday. Want to come to the beach with me and try it out?"

It was an invitation that Encyclopedia couldn't refuse. "You bet," he told Benny.

"Good," Benny replied. "My cousins and I will be there in thirty minutes."

Encyclopedia wasn't thrilled to hear that Benny's two cousins were coming along. He had met Todd and Garth before. Neither of them was what you'd call a quick thinker.

"Mom, is it okay if I go to the beach with Benny and his cousins?" Encyclopedia asked.

"Of course, dear," Mrs. Brown said. "Just make sure to be back by two o'clock—you have a dentist appointment this afternoon."

Encyclopedia quickly changed into his swim trunks and raced to meet Benny and his cousins.

When the four boys reached the beach, only a few other swimmers and surfers were there. The boys locked up their bikes, then dropped their towels near some scraggly pine trees along the dunes. Since it was still early, the trees cast plenty of shade.

"Nice surfboard," Encyclopedia said, taking a closer look at Benny's new board. It was bright yellow with a picture of a surfer riding the crest of a big wave.

"Thanks," Benny replied proudly. "I can't wait to try it out. It has—"

Before Benny could finish, Garth reached down and grabbed the board.

"Catch you later, Benny," Todd yelled as he raced toward the ocean after his brother.

"Hey!" Benny yelled after his cousins. "I didn't say you could try it first!"

Neither Garth nor Todd looked back. Instead, when they reached the ocean, Garth tossed the board into the water, then swam out after it.

"Get back here with my board, Garth!" Benny cried.

Encyclopedia waved his arms, trying to get the boys' attention. But it was no use.

Finally a lifeguard Benny knew noticed the commotion.

"Need some help, Benny?" he asked.

Benny nodded. "My cousins took my new board before I had a chance to try it myself."

"Todd and Garth?" The lifeguard sighed. "Those two have been causing trouble at the beach all summer. I'll get your board back for you." He blew two loud blasts on his whistle.

Garth and Todd hurried out of the water.

"What's up, Dave?" Garth asked.

The muscular lifeguard glared down at him. "Give Benny back his board."

"We were just goofing around," Todd said.

"Give it back now, or I'll make sure this is your last day on the beach!" the lifeguard growled.

Without another word, Garth handed over the surfboard.

"Thanks," Benny said to the lifeguard. He ignored the furious looks that both Todd and Garth were shooting his way. Then he and Encyclopedia raced down to the water.

For the next hour, they had a great time riding the waves to shore. Encyclopedia didn't think about Todd and Garth again until he and Benny headed up the beach toward their towels.

"Your cousins seemed pretty mad at you before," Encyclopedia said.

"So?" Benny shrugged it off. "They'll get over it fast—if they want to try my new board again."

Encyclopedia wasn't so sure that Benny's cousins would forget about the lifeguard's yelling at them. But to his relief, Todd and Garth were both sound asleep on their towels.

Benny and Encyclopedia dried off, then dropped onto their towels too. Encyclopedia checked his watch. It was only a few minutes before noon. He didn't have to be home for another two hours.

Encyclopedia decided to take a nap as well. As he lay down, he could feel the sun warming him. A breeze blew off the ocean. He was just about to drift off when a sound jolted him awake.

"ZZZZZZzzzzzz . . . ZZZZZZzzzzzz . . ."

Encyclopedia groaned. When Benny fell asleep on his back, he snored louder than a chain saw at full throttle.

Encyclopedia poked Benny. "Wake up, Benny. You're snoring!"

Benny grunted, then rolled onto his side. Glad to have some peace and quiet, Encyclopedia closed his eyes and dozed off.

But twenty minutes later, another sound woke him.

"Encyclopedia! My board is gone!"

Encyclopedia's eyes flew open.

"I left my surfboard right there!" Benny exclaimed, pointing to the sand in front of him.

Encyclopedia sat up, blinking as his eyes adjusted to the bright midday sunlight. "Where are Todd and Garth?" he asked, looking around.

Todd and Garth's towels were still on the beach, but the boys themselves were nowhere in sight.

"I don't know," Benny muttered. "They disappeared."

Just then Todd and Garth raced up from behind the dunes.

Benny scowled at them. "Where's my board?" he demanded.

"Oh, man, Benny!" Todd said. "Somebody stole it while you were sleeping!"

"Yeah," Garth said. "When I woke up a few minutes ago, there was a huge shadow coming from behind that tree. I pretended that I was still asleep, and I saw someone grab your board and take off."

"We chased him all the way to the parking lot," Todd added. "But he jumped into his car and drove away before we could get your board back for you."

"That's tough, Benny," Garth said in a sympathetic voice. "Your board was real nice."

Encyclopedia checked his watch again. "Did you say you saw a huge shadow?" he asked Garth.

Garth nodded. "That's right. The thief was hiding behind that tree, making sure we were all asleep before he stole the board."

Benny sank onto his towel. He looked miserable. "I saved my allowance for six whole months so I could afford to buy that board," he said. "Now I'm never going to get it back!"

"Oh, yes, you will," Encyclopedia said firmly. Then he turned to Garth and Todd. "Where did you hide Benny's board?"

How did Encyclopedia know that Garth and Todd were the thieves?

(Turn to page 87 for the solution to The Case of the Stolen Surfboard.)

Solutions

The Case of the Slippery Salamander

Encyclopedia knew that Sam Maine was lying because he told Chief Brown he'd been taking care of "salamanders and *other* lizards for more than nineteen years." Anyone who'd been taking care of salamanders for that long would know that salamanders are not lizards. They are classified as amphibians. Lizards are classified as reptiles.

Sam Maine admitted stealing the valuable new tiger salamander that morning. After he returned Fred to the aquarium, he was fired from his job as caretaker.

The Case of the Banana Burglar

When Encyclopedia examined the first set of paintings, he noticed that the bowl contained seven pieces of fruit—three apples, two pears, and *two* bananas. In the second set of paintings, there were only six pieces of fruit, including one banana. This told Encyclopedia what he wanted to know— that the banana had disappeared between Session One and Session Two, before Pablo arrived.

Monsieur LeBlanc gave Pablo his job back. He also made Bugs Meany clean all the paintbrushes after class for the rest of the summer.

The Case of the Dead Cockroach

Bugs forgot one key fact: Roaches always die on their backs. When Encyclopedia looked in at the dead bug, he could see his shiny brown shell. If the roach had actually died inside the box, as Bugs claimed, the roach would have been lying on his *back* with his legs in the air.

When faced with the truth, Bugs was forced to admit that he'd planned the switch to make the two detectives look bad. The judges disqualified Bugs and his bug from the Insect Race.

The beetle was declared the winner when it reached the outer wall of the ring in one minute and twenty-two seconds.

The Case of the Roman-Numeral Robber

Mr. von Martin made two mistakes.

First, he pretended he didn't know anything about the Roman-Numeral Robber. But when the boys entered the shop, Encyclopedia spotted a copy of that day's *Idaville News* near the cash register. Encyclopedia guessed that the jeweler was lying when he said he hadn't read the articles about the Roman-Numeral Robber. Not only had he read them, the stories had given him the idea to stage a copycat robbery in his own store.

The jeweler made his second mistake when he wrote the date at the top of the note. Instead of writing "XXIV" for June 24, the jeweler wrote "XXIIII." Encyclopedia remembered that jewelers often use "IIII" instead of "IV" when designing watches.

Mr. von Martin admitted that the recent development around the marina had been hurting his business. He'd been hoping to collect insurance money for the valuable watch.

Encyclopedia went home satisfied. He hadn't caught any fish, but he had caught a liar!

SOLUTION TO
The Case of the Runaway Judge

The winner was Roberta Garnet.

Encyclopedia figured this out after he remembered two of Ida Wedgwood's previous jobs: Before becoming a maze designer, she had worked as a jeweler and as a code breaker. Ms. Wedgwood hadn't forgotten to pack her things. She'd left behind the red dress and the calendar open to January as part of the code.

When he looked at the items again, Encyclopedia remembered that the birthstone for the month of January is a dark red stone—a garnet.

The Case of the Peacock's Egg

It didn't take long for Encyclopedia to prove that Wilford's scheme was for the birds. If the con artist had bothered to do his homework, he would have discovered that *peacocks* don't lay eggs, *peahens* do. Furthermore, Wilford was lying when he claimed to have seen the mother bird's beautiful feathers. It's the peacocks who have the beautiful feathers; the female birds are much plainer.

After Encyclopedia laid out the facts, Wilford had no choice. He admitted that the eggs were just ordinary large chicken eggs. He returned Jack's money and stopped selling the phony peacock eggs.

The Case of the Umpire's Error

When the substitute umpire dusted off the plate for the players, Encyclopedia was able to read the lettering on the *back* of the man's T-shirt. But Encyclopedia knew that professional umpires are carefully trained to turn around to face the crowd when they dust the plate. In the major leagues, it is considered bad manners to show your backside to the fans.

Once he had proof that the phony ump had lied about working for the major leagues, Encyclopedia informed the Indians' coach, who stopped the game. The championship match was rescheduled for a later date.

The Case of the Calculating Kid

When looked at from *behind* the desk, the calculator spelled out the numbers 577345. But when read upside down (or from the front of the desk), the calculator spelled out the word "ShELLS." Encyclopedia realized that Kent had managed to leave his parents a secret message: The owner of Shells and More Shells was his kidnapper. The police quickly located the owner, who led them to Kent.

The Case of the Presidential Auction

Gwendolyn forgot one important fact: George Washington had false teeth. Thus, he didn't use a toothbrush.

After Encyclopedia caught her in the lie, Gwendolyn admitted that she'd found most of her "presidential antiques" at a local flea market. Benny and Charlie got their money back, and so did everyone else.

The Case of the Stolen Surfboard

Garth and Todd claimed that they had spotted the huge shadow of someone hiding behind the tree. But when Encyclopedia checked the time, he realized that it was a few minutes after noon—the time of day when the sun is directly overhead. If someone had really been hiding behind the tree, the person would have cast only a very small shadow.

When Encyclopedia confronted the boys with the facts, Todd and Garth admitted that they took the surfboard to get back at Benny. Benny's cousins retrieved the board from where they had buried it in the sand and gave it back to him.

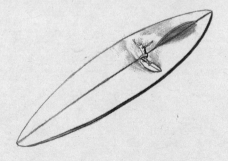